PUP FICTION

Cases from the Files of Sam Spayed, P.I.

April 2012

To my dear friend
Deb Sutherland,

Sherry Gottlieb

With love and woofs!
Sherry
and Sam Spayed

 *Waltsan Publishing*

Cover photograph by Michael Perry

Illustrations by Zoe Z. Spiliotis

Copyright © 2011 Sherry Gottlieb
Published by Waltsan Publishing, Fort Worth, Texas
Imprint: Create Space, Scotts Valley, CA

ISBN: 1461168619
ISBN-13: 978-1461168614

iii —

ABOUT SHERRY GOTTLIEB

SHERRY GOTTLIEB was a bookseller for nearly two decades – she owned A Change of Hobbit in Santa Monica, California, the oldest and largest speculative-fiction bookstore in the world. She is the author of *Hell No, We Won't Go! Resisting the Draft During the Vietnam War* (Viking 1991) – a nominee for the PEN West USA Literary Award for nonfiction. Her first novel, *Love Bite* (Warner Books 1994) was the basis for the 1995 TV movie *Deadly Love*, starring Susan Dey. *Worse Than Death* (Forge/Tor 2000) is a sequel to *Love Bite*.

She lives in southern California, where she was owned by Bunny of Savikko, the Coton de Tulear who inspired this book.

Other Books by Sherry Gottlieb:

Hell No, We Won't Go!
Love Bite
Worse Than Death

DEDICATION

In loving memory of Bunny, my soul dog

CONTENTS

FOREWORD
The Paws Which Refreshes

Sam Spayed came into my life one Sunday in April 1995, a day which began with me driving three hours to desert-rural Lancaster, California, in an uninsured rental car through an unexpected snowstorm to adopt a puppy of an exotic and expensive breed I had never seen outside of the printed page.

Sandra Watt, my agent, had encouraged me to get a dog, promising that it would fill the empty places in my life. Six months before, I'd moved 75 miles to a city where I knew no one, and I hadn't had a Significant Relationship for four years. Although I hadn't had a dog since I'd moved out of my parents' home decades earlier, I was stressed-out and lonely, far from my friends, and I needed the companionship. And Sandy seemed so sure that a dog would help.

After considerable research, both published and anecdotal, I concluded that the perfect dog for me would be a rare breed from Madagascar called the Coton de Tulear. I phoned every Coton breeder in the country at that time, got on waiting lists for a pet-quality female. Coincidentally, one of Sandra Watt's other clients was Dr. Jay Russell, president of the Coton de Tulear Club of America (www.cotonclub.com), and author of *The Lemur's Legacy*. He had been the first to import into the

U.S. this very same rare breed that I'd "discovered" in my research! Jay was more than eager to validate my choice of breed.

Two months later, the day before Easter, I got a call from Coreen Savikko, a southern California breeder who'd just had a last-minute cancellation; she had a 12 week-old female puppy available. I left the next morning, armed with a list of 20 good dog names, all literary, which I had been compiling. There was Dashielle and Toto and Camille and Stel-LA! But I didn't use any of them. Because she was white with pink ears and she bounced and it was Easter Sunday, by the time we got home, she was named Bunny.

From the beginning, Bunny followed me everywhere. If I went into the next room, or even just crossed to the other side of the same room, she came with me. If I went to the bathroom, she insisted on being right next to me. But because she was so small and white, virtually the same color as my carpet and walls, she'd disappear! I would say, "Where's the Bunny?" and, just as suddenly, she'd reappear right next to me, wagging her tail.

Beginning that Sunday in 1995, I had someone to watch out for, someone whose well-being was my job. What a wonderful, new and heady feeling: to be needed! No one had ever really needed me before. Bunny made it very clear that her world revolved around me, that she would do anything to please me. From the beginning, she had always greeted my return home – even if I'd left just to empty the trash – with a welcome so extreme in its enthusiasm that it took a minimum of a minute to complete. Its unmistakable message: Thank

Pup Fiction

doG you're back – now I can breathe again!

Bunny's devotion inspired me to write "The Case of the Missing Mommy" – the first of the Sam Spayed stories that you now have in front of you – for the Coton de Tulear Club of America Newsletter. Jay encouraged me to write more Sam Spayed stories, each of which has run in the CTCA Newsletter. Now, *Pup Fiction* can reach other dog lovers.

Those of you who have lived with a dog understand the bond. No matter what happens, Bunny is right there for me. She doesn't care if I'm sad, grouchy, or not at my most attractive; she loves me more than any human ever could. And she is the repository for all the love I've had to give. Even when I am away from her, she's not far from my thoughts. I know our time together is finite, but I will always have my memories of this wonderful dog. I am glad to be able to share these stories with you.

Update: Bunny died in October 2010, three months shy of her 16th birthday.

"Dogs' lives are too short. Their only fault, really."
–Agnes Sligh Turnbull

Sherry Gottlieb
Mandalay Beach, California

Sherry Gottlieb

THE CASE OF THE MISSING MOMMY

I shredded the overdue notice for a while, then dumped it in the wastebasket. I had worse problems than a past-due phone bill – if I didn't get a new case soon, I'd be out of kibble. I nosed under the desk and found a favorite toy; I tossed the Kong into the air, hoping a Treat might appear, but nothing fell out. I sighed. Treats had been few and far between since I'd gotten my final Bad Boy – thrown off the police force without a pension. They'd said it was because I lifted my leg on the Chief, but I'm certain the real reason they got rid of me was racial: I was the only Coton de Tulear on a force full of German Shepherds and Rottweilers, and my meteoric rise to the Detective Squad ticked off the big dumb pooches who'd been around since Buddy had been in the White House.

Bev, the mail carrier, arrived. I barked and wagged my tail and she gave me a pat on the head and a Treat. It was a good arrangement as far as it went, but that day, it went a little further: Bev brought me a case. She didn't have any details, but a Coton on her route needed help, had to see me right away. I wondered why the client didn't come to me, but then I looked around my office –

not so much as a chew toy or a spare water bowl – hell, I wouldn't come here if I didn't have to. Bev gave me a ride in her Car and let me stick my head out the window.

The client was already waiting at the gate when Bev dropped me off and I could tell right away that she was a rich bitch. She had a jewel-studded collar and a pink bow which read "My groomer loves me," but what really attracted me was her long, freshly washed ivory hair, saucy tail and pouty lower lip. I've always found underbites sexy.

"Mr. Spayed?" she growled softly.

I winced. "Please, call me Sam."

"I'm Bunny of Savikko."

I was right about her status – I knew her family in Madagascar. We sniffed each other. Her butt smelled of flowers, mine of flea powder. Finally, she wagged her tail so I followed her in.

Without hesitation, she leaped onto a black leather couch which matched her black lips perfectly, and told me I was allowed on the furniture. She didn't look at me when she talked, though; her eyes were glued to the front door.

"Would you care for some ProPlan?" she offered.

I tried not to appear too hungry, but I had scarfed the whole bowl before I noticed that she'd merely nibbled at her kibble. Something was bothering her.

I ate her bowl, too. It was puppy formula, which meant she was jailbait...not that I could have done anything, anyway.

Suddenly she ran to the window, tail wagging. She stood there for a few moments, then I saw her tail droop. She came back to the couch and returned her gaze to the door.

"I thought I heard the Car," she explained.

"Expecting someone?" I asked.

The kibble was good, but I still didn't know why I was here. I gnawed at the itch at the base of my tail, then caught the look in her eye.

"Mosquito bite," I lied. "Why did you want to see me?"

"It's my Mommy. She went away, through that door. I want her to come Home."

A missing owner case – that could be worth a pretty pig's ear.

"I don't do strong-arm stuff. If I find her, and she doesn't want to come back, I'm not going to drag her," I warned Bunny. "How long has your Mommy been gone?"

"Forever!" Bunny wailed. "Much longer than Be Right Back!"

"Did she go for a Walk?"

"Not without me!" Bunny said, aghast. "See, my Leash is still by the door. She went in the Car!"

I went over and smelled the Leash. It smelled like Bunny at one end and a Mommy at the other, which didn't tell me much, except that it had been used recently.

"She took you for a Walk today?"

Bunny nodded. "I piddled and pooped, and we said hello to Shanna and Buri. I got a Treat. When we got Home, she went in the Car."

"Is that normal behavior for her?" I wished Bunny'd offer me some more ProPlan. I wondered if it'd be too rude to go into her kitchen and help myself.

"I don't know. I don't understand why she doesn't Stay."

"I have to ask this: Have you ever smelled another dog on her?"

They never want to face that possibility. Sometimes it's worse: Sometimes, they've got a Cat on the side.

I went over to the Mommy chair and sniffed. No Cat. Well, thank doG for small favors.

"Oh no, not my Mommy! Something must have happened to her!"

Bunny was getting hysterical; I had to calm her down. I rubbed her tummy; under the fur, her skin was pink with black spots – a tri-color, passing for white. She spread out all four legs and wagged her tail. But she still looked at the door. I continued to rub her tummy. It felt Good.

"Did your Mommy say anything before she went in the Car?"

I smelled a cow hoof nearby. I stopped rubbing her tummy.

Bunny stuck her pink tongue out over her pouty black lip as she thought. Finally, she nodded. "She told me, 'Be a Good Girl.'"

I looked under the couch. Under the chair. Next to the door. No hoof. Higher. I got up on the couch, sniffed. Closer. Under the pillow? There it was! I grabbed the hoof. What else had the bitch been hiding from me?

But I never had a chance to find out. At that moment, Bunny's Mommy returned, as if nothing had happened. Bunny ran to the door and jumped up and down and wagged her cute little tail and licked her Mommy's face and legs and sniffed at the grocery bags full of Food and forgot I was there.

I slipped out quietly. I marked her mailbox as I left because Bunny obviously wasn't going to pay me. But it wasn't a total waste.

I'd eaten two bowls of kibble – and I had the cow hoof.

SIDNEY AND JULIET

I was sleeping under my desk when Chopin peed on it.

"Hey! What the hell do you think you're doing?" I snarled, looking as ferocious as I could, though that's pretty much a lost cause when you're a 15-pound fluff-ball.

"Oh, sorry, Sam. I didn't see you, so I figured I'd leave you a message," Chopin said matter-of-factly.

I couldn't be too mad. Chopin's probably nine years old, the top dog around here. A Golden Retriever, he seldom has to throw his weight around to get what he wants; you gotta respect him for that. He gives the impression of being deep, often carries two or three tennis Balls in his mouth at a time. He was pretty patient with me back when I was a brash pup, stealing everyone's Bones. He'd never been in my office before, though I'd been working the area for several years – first as a cop, then as a P.I. – and I was kind of flattered.

"To what do I owe the honor of this visit, Chope?"

I cracked open a new box of Treats and tossed over a few. He scarfed them, then went to the door.

— 11

"Let's walk, Sam. Bring the box, will ya? I gotta do something for Sidney; he's miserable. Did you hear him last night?"

"Was that Sid doing all that wailing? Kept me up for hours."

Sidney was Chopin's best friend, another Golden, a few years younger. Even though they had different people, they were practically inseparable.

"Nothing's happened to him, I hope," I said as we left.

Chopin stopped on the landing, cocking his head to use a rear paw to scratch his ear. "Well, you know, Sid's never been...y'know" – his voice dropped to a whisper – "neutered."

I knew. He was one of the few guys in the area who'd been left intact. The people around here were pretty ruthless; I couldn't remember the last time I saw a litter.

I nodded sympathetically. "So, they finally got him last night?"

Chopin shook his head, stopped to read the p-mail on the hydrant in front of my office.

"This way," he told me.

I sniffed the hydrant as I passed; he was trailing Sidney. I knew better than to push – he'd tell me what was going on in when he was ready. I ate a Treat, then another one.

We found Sid outside the Baskin-Robbins store, one of his favorite haunts, but I could tell his mind was elsewhere – there was an entire scoop of strawberry cheesecake Ice Cream melting on the sidewalk and Sidney didn't even notice. Chopin ate it but it wouldn't have killed him to leave me some.

"Hey, Sid," I said. "Whassup?"

He sighed heavily, but didn't Speak. Chopin nudged me to offer Sid the box I'd brought.

"Wanna Treat, Sidney?"

That perked him up. He Sat, drooled. I gave him a Treat. He liked it. Then he took the rest of the box, so it was my turn to sigh heavily.

Finally, Sidney spoke. "It's Juliet. I want her."

Ah, the fair Juliet, a Miniature Poodle who lived over on Montague. She'd shown up as a puppy about six months ago. I'd played Chase with her once or twice at the Park; she was very fast.

"She's not interested, huh? Maybe she's not ready yet, Champ. She's kind of young; you ought to give her some time."

Sidney howled, a mournful cry which startled a lady leaving the Baskin-Robbins into dropping her cone. This time, I didn't defer to seniority – I dove into that sucker myself. Banana nut.

Chopin looked disappointed, although I couldn't tell whether it was because he'd missed the Ice Cream or because I'd been distracted by it.

"Juliet's in heat," he told me, as if that explained everything.

I licked the last of the banana nut off my nose. "Great! Go for it, Sid! Do it for all of us who will never know what it's like. In fact," I suggested to Chopin, "let's go watch!"

"I can't," Sid said glumly, lying down and resting his chin on his front paws. "Juliet won't come Out."

Chopin said, "That's where you come in, Spayed."

"Me? I'm a P.I., not a pimp. You want Juliet to come Out, tell her yourself."

"I did," Sid cried, "all last night. But she can't open the Gate, and neither can I. Her Mommy and Daddy don't want us together because we're not the same breed. She said they want papers for the pups, so they're going to mate her with another Poodle!' He was beside himself.

"You help," Chopin told me, "and we'll pay you."

I'd heard of this prejudice in other places, but this was a mixed-breed neighborhood; I never would have thought that kind of bigotry would show up here. It was pretty disgusting. Also, it's not often I get the chance to help love find a way.

"I'll do it. And you don't have to pay me; I'll take the case *pro bone*. Does Juliet sleep Outside?"

Sidney shook his head. "No, but she stays Out until her people finish Dinner."

I made up my mind. "OK, I've got an idea. Meet me at the lamppost at the corner of Capulet and Montague at sunset."

I used the rest of the day to track down some of

the gang: Truffles, Charlie, and Queen Mab. I'd already explained the situation to them by the time Sidney and Chopin arrived. We trotted down the street to Juliet's house, taking care not to make any noise — we didn't want to alert any people to what was going on. I could've found the house with my eyes closed — Juliet's signal permeated the area with its perfume — so enticing, you didn't need your equipment to appreciate it.

Sidney barked to her as soon as we arrived, and Juliet's yips came back immediately. Sid was about to launch into a big explanation, but I stopped him.

"You want her people to hear? Shush, Sid, or the jig is up." I turned to the others. "OK, here's the plan: we're going to Dig a hole under the fence so these two lovers can be together. Just make it big enough for Juliet to get Out — that's easier than getting Sidney in — and be quiet!"

The others started digging immediately.

"Hold it! Hold it! You should all be working on the same hole!" I rolled my eyes.

Charlie looked ashamed that he hadn't thought of that himself. He abandoned the hole he'd started under a rosebush and moved over to help Chopin, Truffles and Queen Mab next to the gate while Sidney mumbled sweet nothings through the fence to Juliet. I supervised.

It wasn't long before Juliet joined us on the street. She was wearing funny little panties with a hole for her tail; if it was intended as a chastity belt, it left something to be desired – Queen Mab pulled it off in seconds and trotted away with it.

I was wondering how Sidney and his tiny lady love were going to overcome the height problem when the little bitch hopped up on the bus bench and turned her saucy bottom towards Sidney, who quickly jumped on the...opportunity.

Juliet was back in her yard before her people finished Dinner and called her. We even pushed the dirt back in the hole, so no one could tell what had happened.

It didn't remain a secret forever, though.

Juliet's first litter was all Miniature Golden Retrievers with curly hair...and no papers.

WOLF MOON

Every detective has one case he's reluctant to talk about. Sometimes it's because he could never solve it; sometimes, because he could never explain it. My case was the latter. If I didn't have my electric flea trap as proof of Wolf's payment, I'd have long since decided the whole thing had never happened. But I'm putting the Treat ahead of the Trick here, so let me start at the beginning.

I was chewing on a nice beef Bone – courtesy of my neighbor's Daddy, who gets them from Tony Roma's – while trying to remember to not swallow the little chips, a habit which had previously landed me in the hospital for surgery. Due to the Vet's insistence, I'd already given up rawhide chews, but what's life without Bones? Next, she'll be wanting me to give up pig ears! Anyway, there I was, enjoying my Bone, when a 120-pound Bullmastiff pushed his fawn-colored bulk through the office door.

As I weigh a whopping fifteen pounds soaking wet, I rolled over on my back, full submission; he could take whatever he wanted.

The Bone disappeared faster than you can say "Bad

Dog!" (I didn't warn him about swallowing the chips.) My Mommy's slipper, which I'd had since I was a pup, followed the Bone into the gaping maw. But when I saw him eying my bowl of kibble, I managed a warning growl and he suddenly remembered he hadn't come here to eat. He sniffed my butt.

"Are you Thpayed?" he lisped.

"That's a rather personal question," I replied, noticing that his unaltered equipment was about the size of my head. "Call me Tham. What can I do for you, Mr. – ?"

He looked at me blankly. Bullmastiffs are not known for quick thinking. Finally, he said, "I'm Wolf. Tonighth a full moon."

"Uh-huh." I bit at a flea, but the bugger eluded me. "You get those overwhelming urges to Howl, huh? Well, let it out, baby; no one's going to take a rolled-up newspaper to your flank without thinking twice."

It was obvious Wolf wasn't following me. I'd have to slow down and use simpler words. "What do you want me to do about it?"

"Come to my Houth. Thtay. Thomething ith going to happen. I want you to watch me."

Yeah, right. A dog who's bred for protection is afraid of the full moon and wants a bodyguard... so he hires a portable fuzzybutt for the job? It didn't make sense. Maybe it was a set-up; I still owed Rocky the Boxer for the steak I nabbed off his Mommy's plate at the block party last summer. There had to be some safe way to tell Wolf I'd rather go to the Vet's than spend a night with him, but offhand I couldn't think how.

That's when he plopped the electric flea trap on my desk.

"If you Come, you can keep thith." His lisp would be endearing if his voice didn't rumble so much.

I love high-tech stuff, and I certainly had use for a flea trap, but a single night with Wolf could mean I'd never get the opportunity to enjoy it.

"You supply Food, too?"

Wolf nodded. "Thienth Diet. Canned."

That did it. I haven't had canned Food since I was kicked off the police force, and Science Diet was tasty. I agreed to meet Wolf at his place before the moon came up, though I still didn't know what he wanted me to do.

Wolf's people were getting in their Car just as I arrived. Wolf was standing at the gate, watching them go, a pitifully sad expression on his jowly face.

The Mommy gushed, "Oh, look – Wolfie has a little friend! Is that your little friend, Wolfie?"

I wagged my tail and licked her hand.

"Little ankle-biter," the Daddy muttered.

I was tempted to piddle on his Shoe, but didn't want to queer the deal before I'd been fed.

"Honey," the Mommy said to the Daddy, "put out

some food for Wolfie and his visitor before we go."

"His name's Wolf, fercrissakes, Melody – no one names a Bullmastiff Wolfie. If we're late for the movie..."

But the Daddy went into the House, and soon I heard the Can Opener. What a glorious sound! He came back with two bowls, each with an entire can of Food.

By the time I finished eating, Wolf's people were gone, and the pooch was looking dejected.

"OK, Wolfie, what's the agenda?"

Nothing. I sighed and tried again. "What do you want me to do?"

"Wait. Thtay."

OK, I could do that. I sniffed around 'til I found a good spot on the porch, turned around three times, and sat Down. Wolf laid Down on the walkway, blocking the steps so I couldn't leave without him knowing it. Maybe he wasn't quite as dumb as he seemed.

I was almost asleep when the full moon rose big in the sky, so bright I could see a black Cat in a dark window across the street. I glanced at the base of the steps – no Wolf. Well, he had to be around somewhere; I could still smell him. I stretched, scratched at a few itches, ambled over to slurp some Water, then ventured off into the yard in search of my client.

I found him under a tree, whimpering softly. There was something heartbreaking about a dog that big crying.

"What's the matter, boy?" I asked.

"I don't know, but ith been coming all day – thath why I wanted you here. Thave me!" he pleaded.

But whatever was happening to Wolf was beyond my control, beyond anyone's control.

First, the big guy shed all his hair – well, almost all – then he began to writhe, like he had hundreds of flea-bites. His nearly hairless limbs elongated, his forelegs stopping lengthening before his hind legs did – and his bare ears shrunk. I watched helplessly until I could stand it no longer. I buried my head in my paws.

A long time passed, and then I heard Wolf's deep voice. "Tham? Tham, ith over; I'm OK. You can Go Home."

I looked up and saw that Wolf had just emerged from the House. He'd changed. He was standing on his hind legs, eating a raw steak sandwiched between two slabs of cheese...which he held in his Hand. In his other Hand was a can of beer.

The realization hit me hard: Wolf was a were-human, doomed to become a Man whenever the moon was full. He'd asked for my help and there had been nothing I could do to stop it. I hung my head.

But Wolf forgave me. "Ith not tho bad, Tham. I can open the Foodbox by mythelf. You want thome Meat?"

Wow, what a swell fellow, I thought. "Sure, Wolf, I'd love some Meat...and some of that Cheese, too, if you don't mind."

The big guy pulled off a chunk of his sandwich and held it over my head.

"Thit," he told me. Then: "Beg."

It was demeaning, but I Sat. And I Begged. I would have even Rolled Over if he'd ordered me to. But after I finished eating, I went Home, saddened. Wolfie was no longer one of Us; he'd become one of Them.

Sic transit gloria Mastiff.

T.P. OR NOT T.P.

I was having trouble sleeping and decided to go for a late Walk. In the houses I passed I could hear sounds from the odd TV or people snoring, but Outside was pretty quiet, as most of the dogs around here sleep on or near their people's Beds.

I cut down an alley to see if there was any Food behind the restaurant. Last week, I'd found the better part of a pork burrito on the ground, but I wasn't so lucky this time – some idiot had closed the metal lid on the Dumpster. It was just as well – the beans had given me an unfortunate case of gas, so I'd been forced to sleep in the garage that night. Humans are very fussy about smells, I've noticed – no sooner do you get a good stink on than they insist on exile...or worse, a Bath. DoG knows what their hangup is.

I didn't get to eat, but a Cat was strolling past just as I reached the mouth of the alley. He froze when he saw me, arched his back, and hissed – like that's gonna scare me! – so I Barked. Hey, I'm always up for a game. Well, that feline took off like a Cat out of hell – and I was right behind him, all the way down the block. His tail was inches from my teeth as we crossed the street, but I lost him shortly afterwards, when he clawed up and over a high fence. I'm good, but I don't do walls.

But at least the sprint winded me enough so I thought I could probably sleep. I headed toward home, but two doors away, I heard something very odd. Someone was snoring next to the gate. Outside. I went over to investigate. I couldn't see much, but the scent was familiar.

"Psst! Hey, Buri – is that you, man?" My neighbor is a black Lab-mix, whose name, inexplicably, is Japanese for yellowtail fish.

The snoring was instantly replaced with a growl. "Whozat? I'll murderize you!"

A shadow moved, and big white teeth glared in the moonlight. If I hadn't recognized him, I'd probably have piddled in fear at that point, but Buri was harmless.

"It's OK, big fella – it's me, Sam. What are you doing sleeping Outside? Your people go away?"

"No," he said sadly, "they're Upstairs. In Bed. Without me. I've been fired."

He stuck his snout through the wrought-iron gate, and looked at me with soulful eyes. I could tell he'd been crying – his tears had matted his fur. I stepped between the bars – there are advantages to being small – and licked his face.

"Fired? I hope you don't mean they're going to send you to the Pound." Some of the less-enlightened people around here use that place as a threat – and it works, too, because everyone knows that no dog has ever returned from a trip to the Pound.

"Not yet," Buri told me, "but I've been warned. One more slip-up, and it's all over. And I don't get to sleep Upstairs. Even on the rug." He hung his large head. "I've been a Bad Boy," he confessed.

"What'd you do?"

"Nothing. That's the problem. Sometime last night, somebody draped toilet paper all over our yard – the bushes, the trees, the porch – it was everywhere! It took my Daddy all morning to clean it up."

"Surely he doesn't think you did it?"

Buri shook his head. "No, but I didn't stop it, either. I must've slept through it, Sam – or maybe I thought it was the paperboy. I'm so ashamed. What kind of watch-dog sleeps when his property is invaded? A Bad Boy, that's what kind!"

"You gotta redeem yourself, Buri, catch the invaders," I told him. "Then they'll let you back in Bed."

"Will you help me?"

After a quick discussion of fees – we agreed he'd pay me a box of Treats and one shaker of flea powder – I took the case, promising Buri that I'd help him track down the culprits.

I started work the next morning, going door-to-door, asking the neighborhood dogs if they'd seen or heard anything suspicious the night Buri's yard had been invaded. Chloe said the house across the street from hers had been TP'd the previous weekend and she was sure two male humans were involved. Unfortunately, she couldn't be any more specific, but she suggested I talk to Sabrina, which I thought was an excellent idea.

A Bichon, Sabrina is the oldest dog in the area – she has to be at least sixteen. She has only four teeth left, which stick out at right angles, making them virtually useless; her people soften her food with Chicken broth so she can gum it. She goes for a Walk around the block every day before sunset, wearing her babushka, taking slow little steps. The rest of the time, she sits on her porch and watches. Nothing happens in our neighborhood that Sabrina doesn't know about. She watches everything that passes across her line of sight: cars, dogs, Cats, birds, delivery men – if anyone's seen the two male humans, it would be Sabrina.

"Hello, Dollink," she called to me from the porch. "You've come to visit Sabrina, yes? Sit down, bubie. You'd like a Cookie? Someplace around here, I have a Cookie..."

She started wandering around the porch distractedly, searching. There probably hadn't been a Cookie at her house in years.

"No, that's OK, Sabrina; I'm not hungry. Sit."

"How nice of you to come visit Sabrina. I remember when you were just a pup, you came by all the time to give me little puppy kisses."

Actually, I'd been licking the Food which was always stuck on her face, but there was no point in telling her that. I explained my current quest.

"Oh, my dollink! I know those boys. I saw them drape toilet paper all over the yard across from Truffles' – you know, at the Cat house? And I saw the mess at Buri's yesterday when I went out for my morning piddle. Now he has to sleep Outside? Such a shame!"

I listened patiently while Sabrina prattled on about things that had happened before I was whelped because my work was mostly done. Not only did Sabrina know who the pranksters were, but she knew where they lived. When I was able to get a word in edgewise, I thanked her profusely and left.

Buri or I patrolled the neighborhood every night for the next week, while the other kept a watch on one or the other of the boys' houses. Except for chasing the odd Cat or two, we'd had little to attend to, until late one night I spied one of the boys sneaking out of his house carrying two rolls of toilet paper. This was it!

Keeping to the shadows, I followed the kid and saw him meet up with the other boy on the corner.

Buri appeared out of the darkness next to me.

"Should we get them now?" he whispered.

"No. If we catch them red-handed, you'll have a better chance of being reinstated Upstairs."

We tailed the culprits as they entered a yard around the corner from Buri's. While they festooned the foliage, I scratched quietly at a fleabite and Buri licked his privates. The boys finished the first roll of paper and discarded the cardboard core. I always liked chewing TP cores, and planned to retrieve that one when this was over.

"Now!" I barked.

Buri and I ran into the yard, Barking and snarling, lunging at the boys. If they'd known us, they'd have known that neither of us Bites, but the bluff worked. They were terrified.

"Get away! Down! Get away!"

We had them pinned against the wall of the house as lights went on in nearby houses. Humans started arriving in bathrobes and Slippers, including Buri's people.

When Buri's Daddy saw that we had captured the vandals, he told Buri, "Good Boy!"

I stayed in the shadows, content to let Buri take all the credit.

Shortly afterward, the boys' Daddies arrived. They were very angry, and Spanked the youngsters. But that wasn't quite the end. Buri wasn't going to let an entire week spent sleeping Outside go unavenged. As they followed their parents out of the gate, Buri lifted his leg on the youngsters.

Good thing they had some toilet paper.

THE DOGS IN THE 'HOOD

"**S**am! Sam. Hi! Over here! Sam! Sam!"

Behind the chain-link fence was a year-old chocolate Labrador, leaping and wagging his tail so hard he nearly unbalanced himself. He was named Hershey, but everyone referred to him as Pavlov because he drooled whenever he got excited – which was usually.

"Where ya goin', Sam? Do you want to play Chase? I've got a Ball – do you want to play with my Ball, Sam? Or my Frisbee? I've got a Frisbee someplace aroun' – "

"Gee, thanks, Hersh, but I can't today – I've got business to attend to."

Even if I hadn't been on a job, I would have avoided playing with Pavlov – he was nice enough, and really eager to please, but he always drooled on me, which matted my fur and made me smell like a Lab. Also, he'd invariably step on me in his excitement, which could be dangerous, as the kid weighed close to 60 pounds.

"I could help, Sam – I could come with you and help! I'd be a big help, Sam. C'mon, lemme come with you – pul-eeze?"

"Gee, Hersh, I'd love to have you, but your Gate is
— 31

locked," I pointed out. I didn't want to hurt his feelings.

"Oh." He looked down, disappointed, then stepped in a puddle of drool. He didn't seem to notice – but hell, he was a water dog.

"I could try to jump over the fence," he offered, "or maybe I can Dig underneath!"

"I don't think your Mommy and Daddy would like it if they came Home and found you gone, Hersh. I'll tell you what: I'll stop by on my way back and tell you all about it, OK?"

"OK! I'll Stay right here, Sam! I won't move an inch – I'll wait for you to tell me all about it." The big pup Sat, smiling, then stood up again. "I forgot: What are you going to tell me all about when you get back, Sam?"

"About the case I'm investigating, Hersh. Do you

know Fielding?"

"Sure, Sam, I know Fielding! He lives in the House with the iceplant in front. We used to play alla time – Chase an' Ball – an' we'd wrestle – Fielding is really good at wrestling. Did you ever wrestle with Fielding, Sam?"

I'd sooner wrestle an alligator. Fielding was a shaggy, large, Irish Wolfhound who easily outweighed Pavlov. His Mommy had come to me that morning, asking me to find out where Fielding had been hanging out. Apparently, the oversized two year-old had been coming home with bites and scratches – and an attitude – and she was worried about him.

"Have you seen Fielding today, Hersh?" I asked.

His face went blank as another stream of drool lengthened. I'd begun to think he'd forgotten the question when he nodded enthusiastically enough to send the spittle flying through the fence to land on my nose. I tasted it, then wiped it off with my paw.

"I saw Fielding across the street this morning, Sam! He was with some Bad Doggies. I said, 'Hi, Fielding! Over here, Fielding!' but he must not have heard me, because he di'nt Come or Bark or nothin'."

"What makes you think the Doggies were Bad?"

"They looked like Bad Doggies, Sam. They di'nt wag their tails or nothin'."

"Do you know where they went, Hersh?"

"I do, Sam, I can show you! Do you want me to show you, Sam?"

Hersh was getting over-excited again, jumping up

and down; thank doG there was a fence between us.

"I'd like nothing better, but you'll have to just tell me where they went, because I need you to Stay and keep an eye open. Can you do that for me, Hersh?"

"Oh yes!" Pavlov sat...right in the pool of drool. "I'll Stay right here and keep an eye open until you get back from the alley, Sam." He paused. "What am I keeping an eye open for?"

"I need you to let me know if Fielding or the Bad Doggies come back this way, OK? They went to the alley?"

When he nodded again, I ducked, but the spittle just hit me in the middle of the back where I couldn't get at it.

I sighed. "OK, Hersh, you be a Good Boy, and I'll see you later."

The alley was littered with overturned trash cans spilling all sorts of wonderful scents. I'd stopped to investigate one particularly fragrant offering when I heard a menacing, deep-throated growl – not the kind of sound a 15-pound Coton is inclined to take lightly. I looked up, forgetting the heel of French bread in my mouth.

"Drop the bread, Fluffball."

Something was blocking the light from the end of the alley. It smelled like Rottweiler. And Doberman. With a soupçon of Pit Bull. There must've been six or eight of them, baring their teeth. Hershey had been right: They did look like Bad Dogs...and there wasn't one wagging tail in the group. These boys weren't playing.

I dropped the bread, and tried to keep from piddling on myself. It would be fatal to let them know I was afraid.

"Hey, fellas, how are ya? Sorry, I didn't realize the bread had been spoken for – no offense?"

"This ain't your 'hood, Fluffball. What youse doin' here?" The Rottweiler who asked that had a chest wider than I was long.

I opted for honesty. "I'm looking for a friend of mine – big Irish Wolfhound named Fielding. Any you guys happen to see him?"

"Wha'choo wan' the homie for, Fluffy? You a cop?'

"Me? No way. I don't want to make any trouble. His mom wanted me to find Fielding and bring him Home. I'll just do what I came for and leave, OK?"

The Doberman who was blocking the vertical light cackled, "His Mommy sent you? Hey, Fielding – yo mama wants you!"

All the dogs laughed uproariously, except for Fielding, who looked pretty angry. Maybe honesty hadn't been such a hot idea after all. Fielding pushed his way through the crowd and planted a weighty paw on my back until my belly was to the ground. I began to wish I'd brought Hershey – I would have been safer standing behind him.

"Hi, Fielding," I offered up gamely. "Your Mommy's got some new Treats for – "

"Shut up!" he barked.

"Yo mama wants you! Yo mama wants you!" the Pit

— 35

Bull began chanting.

Fielding turned on him with a snarl.

The Pit Bull growled back.

Fielding leapt on him, and as they growled and bit and rolled on the ground, the other Bad Doggies gathered around and cheered on the fight.

Suddenly, I found myself in the clear. I decided that the meal Fielding's mom had offered me for the return of her darling wasn't worth my life so I slipped out of the alley and back down the street while the gang was fighting among themselves.

Pavlov was still waiting at his Gate. As soon as he saw me, he started jumping up and down, wagging his tail and drooling all over again.

"Di'nt you find Fielding, Sam?"

"Yeah, I found him. You were right, Hersh – those were Bad Doggies he was with." I sure wasn't looking forward to telling Fielding's Mommy who his homies were. "He wasn't interested in going with me."

"Did you tell Fielding, 'Come'?"

I shook my head. "No. I didn't think of that, Hersh. But not everyone is as well-behaved as you." Pavlov's tail clanged rhythmically against the chain-link as he wagged it with pleasure. "You're a Good Boy, Hersh. You take care now."

I started to go Home.

"Sam, look!"

I turned back. Fielding was trotting down the block

towards me. He was alone, so I managed, barely, to keep from cowering.

"Hi, Fielding!" Hershey called. "Sam was waiting for you, weren't you, Sam?"

"Shh...sure."

Fielding nodded at Pavlov, which was enough to set off a new drool, then he turned to me. "You shou'nta mentioned my Mommy in front of the boys, Sam – it looks bad, y'know.'

"Yeah. Sorry ab – "

"Never mind. You said my Mommy has some new Treats?"

"Yeah, she said..."

"Thanks for the message," Fielding said as he headed for Home. "See you later."

Not if I see you first, I thought.

But then I realized that Fielding's Mommy wouldn't know that his return hadn't gone quite as planned. I slipped the latch on Hershey's gate. If we hurried, maybe we'd get to Fielding's place before all the Treats were gone.

Sherry Gottlieb

A STAR IS BORED

The House in the Hollywood Hills was impressive, with four massive white columns along the porch. I lifted my leg on the nearest one as I climbed the brick steps, then scratched at the door to be let in. I wasn't sure anyone had heard, so I was trying to figure out how to reach the bell when the door opened, revealing a butler.

"I'm Sam Spayed," I told him. "I have an appointment."

"I'm Michael. Miss Pumpkin is expecting you," he confirmed. "Please follow me."

He led me down a long, carpeted hallway, lined with blown-up photos of some of the biggest stars of film and television, in the roles which had made them famous: Lassie, Morris the Cat, Flipper, Willie the Whale, Eddie from "Frasier" and Babe the Pig. Seemed like Pumpkin had represented every major star since Rin-Tin-Tin; I figured the agent must be about a hundred years old.

The butler pushed open the door to the solarium, with its French doors leading out to the pool and garden.

"Mr. Spayed," he announced, ushering me in.

I almost didn't see her at first, ensconced on a silk pillow in an intricately hand-woven basket. Pumpkin was a tiny thing, couldn't have weighed more than six pounds without the cast on her front leg.

"Forgive me for not getting up to greet you – as you can see, I'm a bit incapacitated, Mr. – "

"Call me Sam. You get into a tussle with a producer?"

She smiled. "A skiing mishap at Vail – Socks Clinton cut in front of me. I've never yet seen a Cat who could ski worth a damn. Please, Sit. What would you like: a Squeaky? a Chewy? Perhaps you'd like something to eat?"

I sat on a brocaded pillow facing the famous agent. "Yes, thank you – a little kibble would really hit the spot."

Michael looked distressed. "I'm sorry, sir – Miss Pumpkin doesn't permit any dog food on the premises. If you'd consider it, I could bring you some poached chicken breast, or bacon, or hamburger."

Pumpkin waved her cast. "Oh, don't be so stingy, Michael, make up a platter with all three. How do you like your hamburger, Sam?"

"Raw will be fine, thanks."

The butler bowed and left.

"Are all those photos in the hallway your clients?" I asked Pumpkin.

She laughed heartily. "How old do you think I am? No, don't answer that! Only the more recent acts are mine; I inherited this agency from my mother, whose father left it to her – which is why it's called The Dynasty."

The butler returned holding a tray, on which was a platter overflowing with luscious-smelling People Food.

"Please, don't stand on ceremony, Sam," Pumpkin said, though I'd had no thought of doing so. "I'll fill you in while you eat. I don't know if you follow the trades, but Buck, who's one of my clients, has been cast as Steve McGarrett in the TV-movie of *Hawaii FidO* which begins shooting tomorrow morning on the CBS lot."

"I thought the series was shot on location," I said around a mouthful of Food. Although I hadn't yet been born when it was on TV, the series often played in re-runs – and I watch a lot of late-night TV.

Pumpkin seemed impressed by my knowledge. "Yes, it was – but the movie script calls for McGarrett and Dano to pursue Wo Fat to the Mainland, so they're shooting the ending first. The cast and crew leave for

— 41

Honolulu on Monday. What I need you to do is make sure Buck makes his 6 a.m. call tomorrow, sober and ready to work. This is his last chance – if he screws this up, The Dynasty's reputation goes out the window with him – and that is something this agency cannot afford."

I nodded. Buck's drinking problem was pretty well known, even outside of the industry. The German Shepherd had lost the lead in *Doggie Bowser, MD* because of booze; eventually they'd recast it with a human. Only last year, he'd made a scene at the Tony awards, screaming that Andrew Lloyd Webber had broken a promise to cast him in his new musical, DOGS, because he'd had "a few beers before rehearsal."

Pumpkin continued. "Buck's just gotten back from the Betty Furred Clinic, and he went straight to the guest suite here, so I can guarantee he's sober at this moment. From now until 6 a.m. tomorrow, he's your responsibility. Whenever you're ready?"

I licked the last of the bacon grease off the platter and my nose. "You can count on me. Which way?"

"I'll take you." She rang for the butler. "Michael, please carry me Upstairs to Buck. Sam, would you like to be carried also?"

"No, thanks. I prefer to walk."

Michael opened the door to the guest suite and carried Pumpkin inside. I followed.

Buck was lying on his back, holding a plush toy shaped like a carrot between his front paws, squeaking it with his teeth. He was surrounded by Squeakies and

Chewies of every description, most of which bore tooth-marks and saliva.

As soon as he saw us, he sat up. "Is this little fluffball my nursemaid? Hell, Punky, she's not even full-growed!"

Pumpkin began to respond, but I motioned to her that I would handle it.

"First of all, Buck, I'm not a she – which you'd know if your sense of smell hadn't been dulled by years of booz-ing. Next, I am certainly 'full-growed' – fifteen pounds happens to be adult weight for a Coton de Tulear. And last, I'm not a nursemaid, I'm a P.I. and bodyguard – and I can handle a sotted Shepherd any day. Now, you got two choices: You can spend a quiet night here with the Squeakies and the Chewies, while I keep an eye on you until it's time to leave for CBS, or you can leave your atti-tude here and we'll go out and do something enjoyable which doesn't involve alcohol. It's up to you; I get paid either way."

Buck's mouth dropped open, and the Squeaky fell out, making a little yip of protest as it hit the carpet. He looked at Pumpkin with incredulity.

"Sam's right, Buck. Until you begin work in the morning, he's in charge. It's for your own good," she added. "Sam, if you need a Car, Michael will drive you. I have a meeting tonight with a rabid entertainment law-yer – I'll see you boys tomorrow at CBS."

She left.

Buck sighed. "Looks like I ain't got much choice. OK, fuzzybutt, let's go paint the town red."

That turned out to be easier said than done. Although Buck was still – barely – a Player in this town, dogs in general were often treated like second-class citizens and we were refused admittance to some of the best clubs in town, even though we slipped Treats to the doormen. Not even Johnny Depp's Viper Room, which had let in a party of pythons as we arrived, would allow us entry. I didn't mind much, having never been interested in the club scene, but Buck was obviously getting depressed about it, and was starting to look longingly at liquor stores. I suggested a movie, but he claimed to have already seen everything at industry screenings.

Michael had been driving us up and down Hollywood streets for hours when Buck said, "Stop the Car!"

Standing on the street corner was a Cocker Spaniel bitch with short fur; she'd seen better days.

Buck went over to talk to her, then brought her back to the Car.

"You Sit up front with the chauffeur," he told me, "and keep your eyes open for cops and paparazzi. And no watching in the rearview mirror!"

So while Buck did his Hugh Grant impression, I sat with Michael, who was kind enough to scratch my ears until the Cocker finished doing Buck and left.

By then, Buck was ready to sleep, so we returned to Pumpkin's house. I didn't quite trust him, though, so I stayed awake all night, listening to the Shepherd snore.

Michael and I got Buck to CBS without any problem the next morning. Hell, Buck even thanked me and gave me an autographed photo ("To my pal, Sam. Best wishes, Buck"). Pumpkin said I could stay and watch the scene, which I did, fascinated by the whole process, although I was so tired, I nodded off as soon as McGarrett and Williams captured Wo Fat and his henchmen.

The last thing I remember was McGarrett's closing line:

"Bite 'em, Dano."

MARQUIS VALUE

I was having a particularly bad bout of the Summer Itchies, and my persistent gnawing at the base of my tail was not only aggravating the condition, but occupying far too much of my time. I couldn't get any work done if I had to stop in my tracks every few minutes to chew ass. So I took the bull by the pizzle and paid a visit to Ida, my groomer, for a thorough Brushing and a medicated Bath.

In general, I am not fond of Baths – getting wet is not my idea of a Good time – but I must admit that after an hour at Ida's, I'd feel like a new dog. The groomer's was also a great place to pick up neighborhood dirt. Although I wasn't actively working a case that day, it be-Hooved any private investigator to keep his nose to the Poop, if you get my drift.

Ida's was jumping...and not with Fleas. There were several other customers in various stages of being spruced up by Ida's team. Ida was tying a pink bow around a worried Beagle who suddenly realized that marked the successful end to her ordeal, so she wagged her tail and gave Ida a kiss. Everyone liked Ida; it was just her preoccupation with Baths and Brushing and stuff like that which gave everyone the willies (except for the

Newfies; Newfoundlands love any excuse to get wet).

One of Ida's assistants was soaking a Persian in a cage in the back sink. The Cat was screaming bloody murder. I grinned.

"Isn't that a lovely sound!" said a nearby voice.

I smelled a familiar dog and turned. Little Lord Montagu was another Coton de Tulear; in fact, we were from the same breeder. Monty affected a British accent, even though he'd been born in Lancaster, California – probably because his Daddy was a Brit. His left front toenails were being filed and buffed; he held out his right paw to Shake.

"Always happy to hear a Cat...er, wauling?" I touched noses with Monty. He was quite active in the Anti-Cat Movement, as I remembered.

"The only thing I like better, Old Sport, is when I've been the one to cause the pussy to cry! So, how are Tricks? You still a private eye?"

Ida put the pretty Beagle in a kennel nearby and gave her a Treat. She helped me up on the table next to Monty and got her Brush.

"When I have a client. I'm between jobs at the moment." I winced as Ida worked on a nasty mat behind my ear. "I don't suppose you know anyone who has need of my services?"

Monty shook his head.

"I do," the Beagle said suddenly.

I turned around to face the kennel, letting Ida work on my rump for a while. "Samuel Spayed, Private Investigator, at your service," I introduced myself to the Beagle.

"I'm Judy. It's not for me, exactly, but for my littermates, relatives and friends. Someone has to save them. You see..." she looked down, ashamed, "...I'm from a puppy mill."

A hush fell over the salon; even the Cat went quiet. The Newf whimpered softly. All ears were on Judy's story.

"It's a terrible place," she explained, "run by a man called The Marquis. He keeps dozens of dogs in cramped cages stacked three and four high in his basement. There are no windows and no sunlight. The piddles and poops from the dogs in the top cages fall on the ones below so they're always filthy and smelly. The Marquis never takes anyone Outside for Walks or to play. Some of the dogs who have been there a long time don't even know how to Walk! No one ever sees the Vet, no matter how sick they are; if they die, he just throws them away and puts someone else in the cage. The only time he gives a puppy a Bath is just before he sells it. The first time I saw grass was when my Mommy bought me," Judy said, her voice catching. "Thank doG my Mommy saved me. Others haven't been so lucky."

Like the others in Ida's listening to Judy's story, I was horrified. I'd heard of puppy mills that bred large quantities of doggies to sell to pet stores and unsuspecting people who thought they were loving breeders, but I didn't know there were any in this area.

"What about the authorities?" Montagu wanted to know. "Why don't they stop this Marquis and shut down his operation?"

Judy sighed. "My Mommy and some of her friends tried that. But they were told that the Marquis wasn't doing anything illegal, so although they were aware of the conditions there, they had no right to punish him.

When I heard Mr. Spayed say he was an investigator, I thought perhaps..." She looked at me hopefully.

"Don't worry, Judy. Sam is going to put an end to the Marquis' puppy mill!" Montagu announced.

I was just about to ask Monty how he thought one 15-pound dog was going to succeed where Human authorities had failed, but everyone in the salon responded with cheers.

"You will, Mr. Spayed?" Judy said, wagging her tail. "If you can just free the other dogs, I can get them to a Rescue group. I just don't know how to get them out of there."

"Montagu will figure out that part – won't you, Monty?" If he was going to volunteer me for this adventure, the least I could do was return the favor.

So there we were, two hours later: two freshly groomed fluffy white Cotons wearing jaunty bandanas being led down the street by a sweet-smelling Beagle in a pink bow.

"It's that house on the corner," Judy said, coming to a complete halt. "There's an entrance to the basement in the back."

I noticed her tail was between her legs and she was shaking.

"You don't have to Come with us if you don't think you can handle it," I told her. The smell of her fear was so palpable, I began to doubt if I could handle it myself, but I'd given my word.

"No, I'll Come. The dogs in the basement won't

know you and it'll be easier to get them to leave if I'm there."

"This liberation will be hard going if the Marquis is home," Monty observed.

Judy nodded. "Wait here. I'll reconnoiter."

Before we could protest, Judy took off towards the house, keeping close to the bushes, her nose to the ground, sniffing as she went. Eventually, she disappeared around a porch and all we could do was wait.

She came running back minutes later. "The Marquis is gone – and the kitchen window is open!"

"To Hounds!" Monty said – an appropriate rallying cry, given the circumstances.

We followed Judy down the street and into the Marquis' back yard. Unfortunately, there was no Doggie Door.

Monty pulled up short. "How shall we get through the window, do you think?"

The open window was at least three feet off the ground, but problem-solving is my forté.

"Monty, you stand under the window with your side against the wall." When he'd done that, I climbed on top of him. "Judy, you get on top of us and see if you can reach the window."

She did as I instructed.

"If you can, go Inside and open the door, OK?"

I felt the weight disappear off my back as Judy went Inside. A minute later, the kitchen door opened. I got off of Montagu and we went Inside. We heard Barking from downstairs. Judy led the way to the basement. The smell got stronger as we went down the stairs – many years of old piddles and poops permeated the cement.

But it was nothing compared to the sight we beheld when we reached bottom: There must have been nearly three dozen dogs of various ages crammed two and three to a cage. Most were Beagles, but there were some Shih-tsus and Cockers and some unidentifiable small-to-medium dogs. They were almost all filthy and matted, except for some puppies in the top cages who were crying in loneliness and fear, having been separated from their mommies far too soon. I smelled sickness there, too. One old male dog was close to death.

While Monty and I began opening latches, Judy explained to all the prisoners that we were friends and we were coming to free them, to take them Outside, and eventually to new Homes where they would be cared for. Those dogs who were freed jumped out of their cages. When all the cages were opened, five dogs remained inside – afraid to come out?

"We'd better hurry," I told Judy. "We don't want to be caught here if the Marquis comes Home."

Judy nodded and went to talk to the dogs still in the cages while Monty and I ushered the others upstairs and out to the back yard.

When we returned, Judy had gotten one of the five out of his cage; he stood shaking on the pavement, his tail between his legs. Judy nuzzled him comfortingly, then said to me, "These three don't know how to walk;

they've never been out of their cages. And Jazz…" she indicated the old Beagle and shrugged.

She didn't have to explain. Jazz wouldn't live long enough to be rehomed.

"Wait here," Monty said. He ran upstairs and returned with several adult females.

After a fair amount of maneuvering, we managed to get all the dogs out of their cages and Monty and his harem picked up all the non-walking dogs by the scruffs of their necks and carried them upstairs and out of the house.

All except for Jazz.

"You need to see the Vet," Judy told him. "The Vet can give you a Shot and make you all better."

"We'll get you upstairs somehow, Old Fellow," Monty said reassuringly, but I wasn't as confident that we'd be able to manage it.

"Leave me," the old stud said. "Get the others to safety. It's too late for me." Jazz lay Down in his kennel amid the poops. "Go."

He finally convinced us. We made sure he had water and food within reach and we left his cage door open in case he changed his mind, then we went to join the other dogs in the back yard.

It was quite a sight: Puppies were romping, playing Chase on the grass. Male dogs were lifting their legs on trees and laughing. Bitches were rolling on their backs on the lawn, tails wagging. Someone had managed to open a faucet on the side of the house and some of the

Beagles were taking turns letting the Water flow over their poop-caked bodies. The joy we saw made it all worthwhile.

Suddenly everyone stopped in their tracks. Dozens of ears went up. Tails dropped between legs.

"He's coming," Judy whispered. "The Marquis' car is on the way!"

I barked, "All right, everyone – playtime's over. Let's line up here behind Judy. Don't forget to pick up the ones who can't walk. Judy, take them through the alley there onto the next block so the Marquis doesn't see them. Monty, you take the rear. Get them to the Rescue group now!"

"But what about you?" Judy asked.

"I have something to do here. I'll catch up with you later. Now, go!"

And with surprising speed, everyone did as they were told. The huge pack of dogs moved quietly out the back gate and down the alley with Judy leading the way and Monty nudging along the stragglers. When the last tail disappeared through the gate, I closed it, then returned to the house to wait.

Two weeks later, I ran into Judy at the Park. She told me that everyone had made it out safely and they were coming along just fine. Ida and her crew had cleaned up all the puppy mill dogs and the Vet had inoculated, dewormed and healed as necessary. Half the dogs had already been rehomed, either to foster or forever care, and the Rescue group was hopeful they'd soon find homes for the rest.

"The Marquis is out of business," Judy concluded. "I heard that the authorities found him in bad shape in his basement. He'd fallen down the stairs and had somehow gotten locked into one of the kennels, covered with filth; he wasn't in his right mind when they took him away. I don't suppose you know anything about that?"

I grinned. "Not me."

"I just wish we'd been able to save Jazz, too," Judy said wistfully. "He deserved to have things go his way before he died."

I thought of the last time I saw the old Beagle in the cage above the Marquis. He was peeing on his captor's head.

"Trust me, Judy: Jazz got the last word."

THE PUSHER'S SON

I nosed the Ball off the top step and gave it a three-stair lead before I raced down to catch it, succeeding two steps from the bottom – not a record, but not bad. I tossed the Ball to the foyer floor and was rolling on my back on it when the entry door opened. There I was, all four paws in the air, rolling on my Ball like a puppy... in front of a Cat! I quickly jumped to my feet and growled – perhaps a bit too little and too late, as the hefty Cat merely stared at me.

"I'm looking for a dog named Spayed," he told me. "I've been told he has an office in this building."

"What makes you think he's interested in being found by a Cat?" I said belligerently.

The Cat took a swipe at my Ball and sent it flying, the implication quite clear that those claws could just as well have been aimed at my head.

"You're Spayed, aren't you, Boy?"

"Neutered. Bitches get spayed," I explained. "And don't call me 'Boy,' Pussy."

I would have chased him if he hadn't been blocking the door. As it was, I didn't have much room in the small

— 57

entryway and he was armed, so I was reduced to verbal bravado.

"You don't want my business? I'll find another P.I." He twitched his tail and turned to leave. "Don't send a dog to do a cat's work, I always say."

"Wait!" I couldn't afford to alienate a potential client, but we weren't exactly off to a great start. "I didn't mean to be rude – "

"– but you just don't like felines. Fair enough. I don't think much of your species, myself, but sometimes you gotta go along to get along, I always say."

It couldn't hurt to hear the Cat out; I could chase him later if he weren't on the level. "Come up to my office."

"Got any Milk or Fish up there?"

Perish the thought. "'Fraid not."

"This'll do fine," he said, plopping down in the only spot where sunshine came through the door.

"So, what can I do for you, Mr. – ?"

"Beauregard P. Buchanan. My friends call me Beau. You can call me B.P." He licked his paw, then washed his face.

"OK, Beepy. What's the haps?"

He looked disdainfully at me and ran a wet paw over each ear before he replied.

"The haps, as you so colorfully put it, has to do with an insidious force which has taken over my once-peaceful neighborhood, a low-life whose mission in life seems to be the corruption of our young, a scourge brought on by liberal owners whose negligence – nay, encouragement! – of licentious debauchery is defiling the very future of the species! I am speaking, of course, of the pusher, the purveyor of pleasure." He was so incensed, he was spitting, and I could smell tuna on his breath.

"Yes, sir, I am speaking of the pernicious drug dealer, the catnip connection! She must be eliminated before she destroys any more lives."

Catnip? Beepy was getting all in a tither over catnip?

"I'm not a hit dog," I told him. "You want someone rubbed out, why don't you do it?"

Besides, we dogs love finding Cats who use the stuff – it makes them real easy to catch.

He suddenly preoccupied himself with searching his tail for fleas. I waited him out.

Finally, he sighed. "I don't want her killed," he said, "just scared out of the neighborhood. I can't be involved because the pusher is...my mother," he confessed.

"Your mother is the catnip connection? Where does she get the stuff?"

"She's the in-house cat at a pet store. Her owners give her drug samples to pass out to the neighborhood cats – you know, the first one's free, that sort of thing? Then, as soon as they're hooked, their owners buy them more. Licentious debauchery, defiling – "

"'– the future of the species.' Yeah, so you said. Your mom's habit doesn't seem to have defiled you much, though, has it?"

Beepy got up and began pacing, his tail twitching to a beat I couldn't hear.

"You don't know what it was like when I was a kitten – all these longhairs coming at all hours of the day and night, using my mom's catnip, lolling around our

60 —

floors and furniture as they slept off their disgusting highs, rubbing up against each other... And the purring! Sometimes she'd let five or six cats in at a time and the purring got so loud, I couldn't think! And Mom used it herself, constantly. It wasn't so bad when she passed out – at least I could nurse then – but it didn't always affect her that way, and more than once, she'd get up and walk away before I'd finished my milk. It was no way to grow up, I'll tell you!"

"Uh-huh, I see. So, even with all those happy pussycats around you, you were never tempted to try the stuff yourself? Never took a little whiff – or whatever you Cats do with it?"

"Sure, I was tempted! Who wouldn't be? To hear them talk of it, catnip is the greatest thing since cream. I was just a little kitten – I didn't want to be left out of the fun. I couldn't resist my own mother, not when I was so young. She turned me on when I was only six weeks old." He hung his head. "Six weeks – imagine!"

I'd begun to suspect what was really bothering Beepy, but if I was right, scaring his mother out of the neighborhood wouldn't make him any happier.

"What happened when you tried the catnip, Beepy?"

"Nothing," he mumbled.

"Nothing?" I repeated loudly. "Didn't you inhale?"

Beepy winced. "Of course I inhaled! I inhaled it, I ate it, I rolled in it. Nothing happened! It had no effect on me whatsoever. I tried it once, but I'm immune, alright? Is that what you wanted me to say?"

It all came clear: Beepy felt inadequate, not fully feline because he hadn't been affected like the other Cats. His own mother gave pleasure to everyone in the neighborhood except him. He figured that if he got rid of the catnip connection, no one would know that he was lacking, but it wasn't that easy. The demon wasn't his mother – or even the drug – it was his own inferiority complex.

"Not all Cats are affected by catnip, Beepy, but perhaps you were just too young. You don't need a P.I.," I told him gently, "you need to come to terms with your own deficiencies, rather than blaming others for them. A good therapist can help you deal with your shortcomings, learn to forgive your mother, and perhaps teach you how to enjoy life more, how to purr. You don't need revenge; you need enlightenment. Go home, Beepy, talk to your mother. Maybe even try catnip again, see what all the fuss is about. Keep an open mind," I added as I nudged him toward the door.

"You think so?" he sniffed.

"I'm sure of it." I crowded him off on the front step and onto the sidewalk. "You ready now?"

He lifted his head. "Yes, I think so."

"OK, I'll give you to the count of three – and no climbing fences!"

I barked three times and Beepy took off with me hot on his tail. I might have caught him, too, if he hadn't scaled a tree and escaped across the roof of a house.

That uptight cat just couldn't stand for anyone to have any fun.

LUCKY DOG

I was between cases so I had time to actually read the morning paper rather than just piddling on it. That's how I found out that Ben's latest human, Roy "Mad Dog" Earle, had been fatally shot by a police sharpshooter during a standoff. Poor Ben had lost more owners than Spïnal Tap had lost drummers – Earle had to have been at least his fourth. Not many other dogs would have crowds waiting for them at the Rainbow Bridge. Ben was a charming midsized mutt with a wide repertoire of Tricks, so there always seemed to be someone ready to adopt him, but he had a reputation for being unlucky.

When I got to work that morning, I found a small crowd of doggies, some with their people on Leashes, blocking the stoop, engrossed in something I couldn't see, but I thought it unlikely that the sign reading "Samuel Spayed, Private Investigator" was what held their interest. When they erupted in barks and applause, I had a pretty good idea what did. I used all 15 pounds of my weight to shoulder a path between a substantial Welsh Corgi named Tubo and a Shepherd mix I didn't know.

Ben was standing on his hind legs on the top step, balancing a Ball on the tip of his nose. In front of him on the stoop was his Bowl. I don't know how long he'd been there, but he'd already accumulated a decent assortment of Bones and Treats. Ben never seemed happier than when he had an audience.

"Show's over, folks – thanks for coming." Ben bowed to the crowd, wagging his tail when he saw me. "Hey, Sam."

"Hey yourself, Ben." I unlocked the door. "My condolences on your loss."

"I'll miss Earle. He was always very Good to me. He fed me Chicken, let me go for rides in the Car and always let me keep the Treats I got doing Tricks – he just took the paper and metal humans threw in. Speaking of Treats, help yourself, Sam." He put his Bowl down inside the office and shoved it towards me with his nose. "But best of all, he took me for Walks in the rain. I've always loved piddling in the rain," he sighed.

I nodded and took a Dentabone to chew on while we talked.

"What're you gonna do now, Ben? Got another human lined up?"

Ben sniffed the carpet, raised the nap with his front paws, then circled a couple of times and laid Down.

"That's what I wanted to talk to you about, Sam."

"*Mi casa es su casa, amigo.*" I meant it, even though I didn't know what it meant. "You can Stay as long as you need to."

Ben looked touched but sad, then he began to Howl.

"The first few times I lost my human, I said, 'It could've happened to anyone,' but I've lost half a dozen of them now, Sam. It has to be because I'm a Bad Dog."

Theology has never been my strong suit, but I also knew that Ben was a Good Boy.

"It's not you. I don't know what it is, but it's not you. You'll get a new human – maybe even a kid."

Getting adopted by a kid was a dream for most doggies. Children spent significant amounts of time Playing, often with Balls or Sticks, and Running, and they were usually pretty good about bringing their dogs along – and even if they did forget to feed the dog once in a while, their parents usually reminded them or took care of it themselves. But more importantly, at least for poor Ben, they almost always outlived their dogs.

"DoG, no! Much as I'd love to have a kid, I can't risk another adoption, Sam. I'm going to find my real Mom."

I nearly choked on the Dentabone. Although I was willing to help Ben any way I could, he was a Heinz mutt – 57 varieties – with no papers, no clear clues to his ancestry.

"Cheese, be realistic here! And even if we could find her – a very big 'if,' I might add – she's bound to be a very old dog and probably wouldn't welcome the return of a prodigal pup."

But Ben wasn't to be dissuaded by logistical realities or "you can't go Home again" arguments.

"I don't plan to move in with her," he said, although I could see in his eyes that that was exactly his fantasy.

He was tired and depressed and he wanted to be taken care of.

So we emBarked on a campaign, posting flyers with puppy and adult pictures of Ben – "Is this your son?" – and visiting every bitch of the right age and size.

One day, after dozens of dead ends, I saw an elderly Jack Russell mix behind a screen door and showed her Ben's pics, asked if she recognized him.

She had cataracts, but she sniffed the flyer, then said, "My baby! Where is my baby?" She was so excited, she piddled where she stood, wagging her tail so hard she lost her balance and plopped right into the pee.

I couldn't believe I'd actually found her. "Wait here," I told her. "I'll be right back with your baby!"

It took me a little while to find Ben – he was near the school, doing Tricks for kibble in front of a substantial crowd. As soon as he'd heard that I found her, he took off so fast, he left his audience – and his Bowl – behind.

As he ran up the front lawn to her screen door with me right behind him, I could hear the old terrier still calling, "My baby – where is my baby?"

"Here, Mama, here I am!" Ben said, his tail high.

But his tail drooped when the old girl's Mommy gave her a pat on the head and a well-chewed plush Squeaky Toy and said, "Here's your baby, Princess. Here's your baby right here."

We never found Ben's real Mom, and eventually Ben decided it was time to move on to look for her. With his Tricks, he'd never go hungry, but would he ever find happiness again?

I needn't have worried.

It was two seasons later when I received a p-mail from my old friend:

Dear Sam,

I hope this finds you in good health. I never did locate my Mom, but I made my way to Hollywoof, where I immediately found work doing Tricks for the movies, performing under the name of The Amazing Ben. The director of my last film has two kids who love me and I love them. They've asked me to move in with them, and I've said yes. Anytime you're near Hollywoof, look us up – there'll always be a Chicken in the pot for you!

Ben

Hollywoof, USA

Sometimes Life just works out. The Amazing Ben had enclosed a photograph of himself with two kids, a boy and a girl about 9 or 10 years old – he was grinning from ear to ear. He also sent passes to his new movie, "Peeing in the Rain."

THE MYSTERY AT MIDNIGHT

I was sound asleep in my favorite position – belly up, all four paws spread-eagled, head hanging over the edge of the couch – when I was suddenly awakened by the most unearthly howl, a sound of such unremitting agony and terror that the fur on the back of my neck rose and my tail tucked itself between my legs.

I rolled off the couch and shook myself, but the sound which had awakened me had stopped. I ambled over to the bowl for some Water, just beginning to think the heart-wrenching sound was something I'd merely dreamed, when I heard it again. It seemed to be coming from the direction of the Park, but I couldn't be sure so I pushed open the flap on my Door and went Outside to better assess the situation.

The full moon was bright as I marked my perimeter, waiting for the sound to repeat yet again. I didn't have long to wait. The doggie (for it was clear now that the sound was canine) cried his most pitiful wail, a sound which carried throughout the neighborhood. Heidi and Rumpy, the twin bassets on the next block, apparently thought it to be the overture to the Full Moon Opera, so they began a chorus of supporting howls. Heidi and Rumpy never missed an opening – whenever a siren wailed past, they always joined in.

I heard a window open. A man yelled, "Shut up! Damned dogs!"

The bassets stopped almost immediately, but the more distant doggie howled again. I didn't think his was a song to the moon, however; the dog was obviously overwhelmed by loneliness and, perhaps, grief – his human or his mate had left, either temporarily or permanently. To us dogs, it's much the same thing; we're not known for our sense of time.

After a while, the heartbreaking howls of deep loss were spaced further apart; then they stopped completely. The poor canine had apparently worn himself out and had finally fallen asleep. Perhaps the rest of the neighborhood could sleep now, too.

I went back Inside, raised the nap on the carpet with my front paws, and laid Down. In the morning, I would start asking around, see what I could find out.

"Cheese, Sam, did you hear that ghastly noise last night?" Snookums stood on the back of his couch and leaned his front paws against the window screen to talk to me.

"Yeah, they could probably hear it all the way down at the Pound," I said. "You have any idea who it was?"

Snookums snurfled, as Pugs are wont to do. "Nope. Sure sounded miserable, though, didn't he? My Mommy was so scared, she kept me with her in the bedroom and didn't open the door until sun-up. I couldn't get to my kibble or my Water. When she fell asleep, I piddled in her closet," he confided.

The Pug had some unresolved issues with his Mommy-person, but I wasn't about to get involved in trying to straighten them out. I'm a private investigator, not a therapy dog.

I checked the p-mail on the hydrant in front of the stoop. "Chloe was by here this morning, Snook?"

"Yep. She said she heard that the howling was coming from over near The Moors."

The Moors was an apartment complex on the other side of the Park, but it was unlikely that the little Bichon was right about the howling emanating from there. The place had a strict no-pets policy, and although it was rumored that there were Kitties there, we dogs are a lot harder to hide from a landlord. Duke, the Doberman who now lives with the mobile groomer, lived in The Moors when he was a puppy, but the landlord found out about him and gave his humans an ultimatum: Either Duke goes or they all do. Duke's owners didn't think twice – they gave him to the groomer. It turned out all right for Duke – unless you count the fact that he had to take Baths far too often for his tastes – but I think he was still hurt that his humans didn't move out with him. It's hard to understand some people, you know?

I decided to head over to Chloe's house, a popular

destination for all the neighborhood doggies, because her Mommy-person roasted a Chicken every week just for Chloe and her guests, and for their ancient but vicious Kitty. The little Bichon didn't make friends easily, but once you got on Chloe's good side, you could get Chicken every time you visited — as long as you didn't mind getting nailed by a Cat when you weren't looking. There are no unmixed blessings anymore, you notice that?

Joey was leaving Chloe's just as I arrived.

"Yo, Mister Spayed!" Joey said when he saw me. "How's it hanging, bro?"

"Low and heavy, Joe. How's yourself, m'mutt?"

The Aussie Heeler licked his lips, then grinned. "Got some Chicken juice on my muzzle and managed to dodge the pussy. What could be Bad?"

Sounds like I just missed the Chicken handout, much to my disappointment. I looked pointedly at Chloe, but she didn't get the hint.

"That howling last night was pretty Bad," I observed.

Chloe nodded. "Everyone in the Park was talking about it this morning. Sage said there's a doggie in The Moors." While Joey stepped into the iceplant and left a Poop, she continued, "If you want to go over and check it out, Sam, I'm up for another Walk."

"Not me," said Joey. "It's almost time for breakfast." He waved his tail and left.

I usually work alone, but when Chloe promised

Chicken when we got back, I agreed to take her along.

When we reached the far end of the park, we saw Sammy Outside taking a Piddle. Sammy is very old and doesn't walk very far anymore, but her house was in Sherlock Homes, right on the edge of the park, which was nice for the old girl because it kept her right in the thick of things from the comfort of her patio. It occurred to me that Sammy might know something about the dog from last night; I said as much to Chloe, so we changed course toward the old black dog.

"Howdy, Miss Sammy," I said.

"Who's that?"

"It's Sam Spayed, Miss Sammy – and Chloe. You remember us from the Doggie BBQ in the Park when Chloe's Mommy gave us all Chicken?"

Sammy sat down with a sigh. "Yes, Chicken. I remember Chicken. How are you both?"

After an exchange of pleasantries, I mentioned the howling from last night. "I don't suppose you know anything about it, Miss Sammy?"

"Oh, my, yes. I know everything about it," she said confidently. "Bayou – that's the poor dear who was howling – a perfectly charming bloodhound with great slobbery jowls – lives right next door to us."

"He lives in Sherlock Homes," Chloe asked, "not at The Moors?"

Sammy looked at Chloe as if she didn't have the brains doG gave an Afghan and said patiently, "No, dear. Doggies aren't allowed in The Moors. The last doggie who lived there was Duke, the groomer's Doberman. Bayou moved in last week, right next to us in Sherlock Homes – he's the Baskervilles' hound."

Well, that solved the question of Who.

Chloe asked, "Why did the hound howl?"

Sammy had nodded off to sleep, but by then, I knew the answer, so I said to Chloe, "First, tell me: Why do you think Bayou stopped howling this morning?"

Chloe thought about it for the longest time, but she wasn't the brightest pup in the litter and if I waited for her to figure it out, I might never get any Chicken, so I told her:

"The hound didn't howl this morning because the Baskervilles returned from wherever they'd been all night, so Bayou no longer mourned their absence. Since they were new to Sherlock Homes, the hound was insecure about being left alone in an unfamiliar place."

"That's right," Sammy said, waking just in time to hear the last of my explanation. "I heard their car return shortly after dawn today." She rose awkwardly to a standing position and began toddling off toward her house. "I'm sure Bayou didn't mean to disturb anyone. He's quite a dear, you know."

When she was gone, I said, "Well, the mystery of Sherlock Homes' hound of the Baskervilles is solved. How about getting some Chicken?"

DOGS OF WHINE AND ROSES

I rinsed the Fleaz-No-Mor out of my fur and stepped out of the shower, then shook out all the Water. It was only when I realized that I had once again soaked my towels before using them that I remembered I was supposed to shake inside the shower. If my Mom had been around, I would've gotten a Bad Dog for sure. I rolled around on my back on the bathroom carpet – which wasn't appreciably drier than the towels, come to think of it – then checked out my reflection in the mirror. I was still as handsome a Coton de Tulear as ever graced the private investigator trade, but I had to admit that the world-famous Sam Spayed was getting a little "fluffy" around the middle. I was going to have to cut back on the pig ears.

It was a beautiful day, so I decided to take the scenic walk to my office, along the alley behind the strip mall, where one could frequently find discarded burritos and pizza, past the open back door of the video store where the store's Cat usually sunned itself – there it was! I rushed the Cat with an exaggerated Growl-Woof which sent it fleeing to the interior of the store; I didn't bother to pursue because the Cat's human didn't take kindly to that.

I stopped to read the p-mail at the corner lamppost – Chang had been by that morning, as had Sage (who, apparently, was feeling a little under the weather), and a dog whose signature I didn't recognize, but he was middle-aged, neutered and in good health. He was also very tall; standing on my back paws to sniff, my nose was still several inches below his posting. I wondered if he were still in the neighborhood, but I didn't have to wonder long.

Passing the driveway to the yard with the summer Barbecues, I was hit broadside and barreled over by a truck at the same time I heard a woman shriek, "Stop that dog! Come back here, you!"

I untangled myself from an azalea bush and realized that I hadn't been hit by a truck at all, nor was I the dog she wanted stopped – the solution to both of those was the brindle Great Dane booking at top speed down the block, trailing in his wake a rose-colored flag, as well as the screaming woman in robe and Slippers.

Dusting myself off, I said, "Allow me, ma'am. Sam Spayed at your service," and without waiting for her reply, I hauled tail after the Dane.

Those big dogs have it all over us little guys in stride – hell, I must've taken six steps to his one – but I was the fastest dog in the neighborhood since the Whippet moved away. I caught up with the Dane near the Park, stopping him by running between his legs so he tripped over his own Paws and fell in a heap tied up in rose-colored silk.

"Oh, noooooo," he wailed. "Look at it – it's torn! Now I'm really going to be a Bad Dog!"

He laid the silk thing on the ground and nudged at it with his huge snout, as if trying to push it back together.

"What is that, anyway?" I asked, sniffing it. It smelled of soap and the lady from the Barbecue house. There was a prodigious amount of dog slobber on it.

"It's a teddy," the Dane howled, "and it's ruint!"

I'd had a Teddybear when I was a pup, but it didn't look or smell anything like this, and I said so.

"Bears don't wear teddies," the Dane said, aghast. "Ladies wear teddies. And bras. And stockings. And – "

he added with a moan of pleasure, " – panties."

The big fella had a fetish. I'd seen it before. They start out sniffing a Slipper when they're pups, maybe chewing on a sock or a Shoe. Most of them outgrow it; some don't.

"Your Mom looked pretty pissed about you taking her teddy," I told him.

"She's not my Mom. My Mom won't let me have any more lingerie. She put locks on her drawers, keeps her laundry in the closet, and won't let me in the bathroom when it's hanging up to dry," the Dane sighed. "So I'm reduced to getting it where I can. This was a particularly nice piece," he nudged at the rose-colored silk again. "But now, when I take it back, the lady is going to still be mad at me 'cause it's torn."

I refrained from pointing out that she probably wouldn't be too thrilled with all the dog slobber, either; the Dane seemed distressed enough as it was.

"What's your name, big fella?"

"Borge." He pronounced it Borga.

"Sam Spayed." We Shook paws.

"Borge, you plan to return this...teddy to the lady?"

"I can't now, I told you. It's ruint and she'll be mad and she'll get my Mom's phone number off my collar tag and she'll call my Mom and she'll tell my Mom I'm a Bad Dog and my Mom will yell at me."

Borge began to sob...into my fur. What did he think I was, a hankie?

"Maybe she'll even send me to the Pound!" he added between sobs.

I tried to extricate myself, but I think the Dane's massive head alone weighed more than I did, so I resigned myself to being covered by slobber until I could get home to take another shower.

"Why did you take the teddy if you were just going to return it?"

"I wasn't gonna chew it, honest! I was just smelling it when the lady saw me and...I don't know what came over me. Instead of rolling over, I ran. I always try to return them," he said defensively. "I'm not really a Bad Dog. I've got a little problem is all."

I could tell Borge was full of remorse, but whether it would be sufficient to prevent this from happening in the future, I wasn't so sure. He couldn't even admit to being a Chewer.

"OK, big fella, I'll tell you what I'm going to do. I'm going to take the teddy back to the lady at the Barbe – " I stopped before I finished the magic word, " – at the house, and I'm going to tell her that I was able to recover her lingerie but that the perpetrator got away."

Borge snurfled. "You'd do that for me?"

I nodded. "On one condition."

"Name it!"

"You have to get some professional help – maybe go to a behaviorist or group therapy or something."

"I will! I'll do that!" Borge slurped his huge tongue over my face so that all my fur matted with slobber. "I can't thank you enough, Sam Spayed – I promise you won't regret your trust in me!"

And I never have. I pass the Kennel every day on my way home from the office, and I frequently see the Dane attending meetings there.

"Hello, my name is Borge, and I'm a Chewer."

"Hi, Borge!" comes the chorus.

THE MALTESE FROG

She sashayed into my office, her black-and-white hair in a fashionably curly bob rather than the long silky tresses traditional with Shih-tzus; I knew right away she was no ordinary bitch.

"Are you Miles Archer?" she asked me.

I'd never heard of him. "Who?"

"Never mind," she said. "You're an investigator?"

"I am. Samuel Spayed, P.I., at your service; you can call me Sam. What can I do for you, Miss..."

"O'Shaunessey. Sushi O'Shaunessey. I need you to help me avoid some dogs who want an ornament which is coming into my possession."

I leaned against my desk. "Why don't you tell me about it, Miss O'Shaunessey?"

She got closer.

"Sushi," she said in a husky little growl.

"The 'ornament' is raw fish?" I asked, confused.

She rolled her eyes impatiently. "I'm Sushi. The ornament is a Squeaky I've arranged to...acquire. It's very rare, and it's taken me a long time to get it. There are some who would like to take it away from me. I'll pay you handsomely to protect me from them until I can get safely away with the Squeaky."

"How handsomely?"

"This is just a retainer," she said, plopping a bagful of pigs' ears on my desk.

"That's good – that's very good. But I have to see this Squeaky – I can't guard what I can't recognize," I told her.

She looked down. "I don't have it yet – I'm getting it tonight. It's a frog, about two mouthfuls big – "

Fortunately, we had about the same size mouths. "What makes this frog so rare?"

"Its squeak is as unique, as delightful, as the day it was made – even though that was many lifetimes ago. It belonged to The Maltese," she added. "Have you heard of him?"

Of course I had. The Maltese was legendary. His owners had spared no expense on his Food, Treats, and toys. His sweaters were hand-knit to his measurements, his Squeakies custom-designed for his bite; rumor had it that they were flavored with Chicken or Bacon, and never lost their flavor or their squeak.

"I heard that all the Maltese's Squeakies were cremated with him," I told Sushi. "How did you get one?"

She sighed. "It's a long story, Sam. The Maltese Frog is the only one of his toys to survive the funeral. I've tracked it from Singapore to Istanbul to Cairo, obsessed by nothing else. Now I'm finally about to lay my paws on it and I don't want to lose it. Even as we speak, I've been followed. Look out the window," she suggested.

I went over to the window and stood on my hind legs so I could peer over the sill. On the street below was a skinny young mutt leaning against a fire hydrant.

"You talking about the gunsel with the notched ear?"

"That's him," Sushi hissed. "His name's Wilmer. He works for Kasper, the Fat Dog. Kasper and I were partners once. We're not anymore."

I'd had a feeling this bitch couldn't be trusted, but I trusted her bag of pigs' ears. And if I helped her, maybe she'd let me play with her Squeaky.

"Where do you pick up the frog?"

"It's coming in on the *Chien Andalou* at sunset tonight."

"OK. I'm gonna go down and have a talk with Wilmer there. When you hear me Bark, you slip out through the back. I'll meet you at the dock at sunset."

I snuck up behind Wilmer and barked loudly. Just as I'd suspected, he folded right away, went belly-up in submission.

"Take me to the Fat Dog," I told him.

Wilmer whined piteously, but didn't move.

"Now!" I barked.

He scrambled to his feet and started trotting down the street, stopping every few blocks to glare back at me.

"Keep on riding me and they're gonna be pickin' my teeth outta your ass," he growled.

I grinned. "The cheaper the crook, the gaudier the patter."

The name "Fat Dog" didn't do justice to Kasper's stature. He was the most formidable Shar-pei I'd ever seen, and his tiny ears almost disappeared in the deep folds and wrinkles of his bristly coat. He wasn't particularly large, but he radiated an aura of strength and self-confidence which brooked no challenge. When he smiled, the temperature in the room dropped.

"You like to talk, sir?" he asked me.

"Sure, I like to talk."

"Well sir, I'll tell you right out: I'm a dog who likes talking to a dog who likes talking."

"Swell. Will we talk about the frog?"

"That depends. Are you working for Miss O'Shaunessey or for me?"

"I'm working for myself. Say I can lay paws on the frog, Fat Dog – what's it worth to you?"

"Well sir, I think I can manage to trade, say, your weight in steaks. What do you say to that?"

Jeez, I had the wrong client – steaks beat pig ears, paws-down. "I'd like to taste one before I decide."

"Certainly. Wilmer, bring our guest a steak."

Wilmer growled, but disappeared into the other room. He returned with a rib eye – no bone, but great flavor. I dug in, but was only partway through before I started to feel dizzy and my vision clouded. I realized that I'd been drugged just as I passed out.

When I awoke, I was alone and the sun was almost down. I had to get to the *Chien Andalou*!

I ran all the way to the docks, but I was too late: The ship was there, but it was completely ablaze. There was no sign of Sushi O'Shaunessey, Kasper the Fat Dog, or Wilmer the Gunsel. If one of them hadn't gotten the Maltese's frog before the fire started, it was history now. I overheard someone say that even the Captain's dog, Jack, was missing in action.

I went back to my office.

I was putting the bag of pig ears in the desk when the door opened and a wire-haired dachshund staggered in with a newspaper-wrapped package in his mouth and died, right there on my floor. It was obvious from his wounds that he'd been attacked by at least one vicious dog.

When I opened the package, I realized the daschsie must be Jack, from the *Chien Andalou*. I now had the frog, but there wasn't time to taste or squeak it. Whoever killed Jack might have followed him here.

I rewrapped the frog, took it out and buried it where it was unlikely to be found by a dog: behind the Vet's office.

Unfortunately, I'd been followed. I'd barely left the block when I found myself surrounded by Kasper, Wilmer, and Sushi. Wilmer had blood on his muzzle; ten-to-one it was Jack's blood.

"Let's do some business, sir," Kasper said. "You have something I want."

"Maybe, but I'm not trading it for a bunch of drugged steaks," I told him. "And I'm not afraid of your gunsel, either. I'm not as easily killed as the Captain's Jack was."

"What about getting it for me, Sam?" Sushi rubbed up against me.

If I hadn't been neutered, it might have been more effective, but the point remained that I'd taken her retainer, so she was my client, no matter what else was in the offing.

"If I give it to you here, these guys are gonna take it from you," I pointed out.

"I want Kasper to have it, Sam. He's paying me very well for the Squeaky."

So, she spent all those years looking for the frog, only to trade it for a few pounds of steak. Well, it was her choice.

I took them back to the Vet's office – noting with satisfaction that Wilmer piddled on himself as soon as he smelled where we were – and dug up the bundle.

Kasper tore off the newspaper and bit into the frog. It didn't squeak. Not one bit.

But Kasper did.

"It's a fake! This isn't the Maltese Frog – it doesn't squeak!"

He dropped it, so I went over and tried. He was right – the frog had no squeak – and it wasn't flavored, either. They'd all been scammed – maybe it had been switched in Singapore, or Istanbul, or Cairo, but now there was no way of telling if the Maltese Frog actually still existed.

While they were fighting about who'd screwed up – and, more importantly, who owned the steaks – I picked up the fake frog as a souvenir and left.

As I turned the corner to my office, Zoloft saw me. "What's that you've got?" he called.

"The stuff that dreams are made of," I replied.

Sherry Gottlieb

The End

Made in the USA
Charleston, SC
14 March 2012